The Fever in the Water

Greenland Missing Persons #4

featuring Constable Petra "Piitalaat" Jensen

Don't miss novella #5 in the
Greenland Missing Persons series
The Winter Trap

Author's Note

The settlement of Ingnerssuit does not exist, and neither does the Greenlandic police force use a shaman's to help solve cases. But, if you want to know more about Constable Petra Jensen's early career, then this novella will add more background to her story and the characters with whom she interacts, including some who may be familiar if you have read any of my other stories set in Greenland.

Chris
August 2020
Denmark

The Fever in the Water

Greenland Missing Persons #4

Part 1

Sergeant Gaba Alatak raised his voice above the crash of waves against the bow of the red-hulled police cutter *Sisak III* as he addressed his team. Atii and I stood just behind them, fiddling with our gear on the rear deck. I struggled with the Velcro straps of my ballistic vest, trying to get a proper fit, until Atii turned her back on Gaba's Special Response Unit to help me.

"The strap was bent back on itself," she said, shifting her feet as the cutter rolled slightly to port. "It's tight now."

"Thanks," I said.

"Are you okay, P? You look a little green. Is it the boat?"

I paused to work some saliva into my mouth to unglue my tongue, and said, "I'm not used to this."

"To what? Working with SRU? Neither of us are."

"Then why are we here?"

"Duneq said there were women and children in the house. He said Gaba needed female officers. I guess we were available."

"I guess," I said, wondering in part how Atii could be so cool when I wasn't.

I let my mind wander to earlier that morning. Sergeant Duneq had pulled Atii and I off our regular activity for the day and driven us to the airport where Gaba and his team were waiting.

"I told them you weren't ready," he said, looking at me in the rear-view mirror, before flashing through a roundabout, braking into the curve and accelerating out of it. He could have been talking to both us, both newly trained, both equally green, but it was the look that confirmed it.

He was talking to me.

"Paamiut police have officers on the scene, at the dock in Ingnerssuit, but they're waiting for SRU before going in." Duneq paused as he braked at the next roundabout. He stopped the patrol car for a cyclist, adjusted the fold of his belly pressing against the steering wheel, then accelerated. "Eqqitsiaq Kuannia is sixty-nine years old. Residents in Ingnerssuit say he's gone nuts, and he has a gun, and he won't let his wife or daughter out of the house. The daughter has three children. They are also in the house." Duneq slowed into the long curve of the road at the end of the runway. "That's all I know. Gaba will tell you the rest."

I felt the first flutter of nerves in my stomach as Duneq parked outside the main entrance to Nuuk airport. This wasn't the usual assignment he gave me, the kind I often felt he used to punish me. This was different, and I wondered, just for a second, if he was trying to protect me. Sergeant Duneq – or *Jowls* as I called him – was my supervisor. He often threw obstacles in my way, pretending they were vital to my training, now that it was over, so that I might get as much experience as possible in as short a time as possible. Which could easily be translated to more work and fewer days off. But this was different. He looked concerned, and I think that was what worried me the most.

The final straw was when he told me to be careful, just before Atii and I got out of the car.

"Did you hear that?" I said, as Atii tugged me through the main door of the airport and into the waiting area. "He said we should be careful."

"We'll be fine," Atii said. "Don't think about it."

Of course, *not thinking about it*, was like not breathing. I *had* to think about it, teasing apart all the different emotions associated with Duneq's uncharacteristic concern, right up until the airport gate, where Gaba and his team were waiting.

"You won't be going in," he said, bustling us out of the door and into the Air Greenland *King Air* light aircraft waiting to fly us to Paamiut. "But I need you close, and I need you focused. Understand?"

I remembered nodding, but little else. It was Atii who guided me into a seat on the tiny plane, telling me to buckle up as Gaba dumped bulletproof vests and helmets into our laps. I remember clutching them from take off to landing, before dressing on the boat.

"Hey." Atii tugged at my vest, jolting me back into the present. "You with me, P?"

"Yes."

"You're going to be fine," she said. Atii laughed and squeezed my arm. "Is this the same Petra who chased a polar bear with her pistol in Qaanaaq?"

"That was different."

"How?"

"It just was," I said. "This is more real, somehow."

I reached out to clutch the cool railing as *Sisak III* ploughed through another wave. Atii did little more than shift her feet to find her balance. The wind played with her long fringe and I waited for her to say something, more reassuring words, but we were out of time. Atii pointed over my shoulder, towards the bow of the boat, and said, "We'll be there soon."

My breath caught in my throat as Gaba strode across the deck, stopping beside Atii and me.

"Your hair," he said, pointing at my ponytail. "Make the knot lower so it fits under your helmet." I fiddled with the elastic in my hair as he studied my vest, tugging at the same straps Atii had helped me with. "You seem nervous, Constable."

"She's fine," Atii said.

"Okay," he said, slowly, before spinning me around to check the back of my vest. "Let's see."

I felt the rough brush of his strong hands, curious that my previous thoughts about Sergeant Gaba Alatak, the less than professional kind, were quashed by the threat of impending action. Atii seemed far more confident and made a show of enjoying Gaba's inspection of her gear once he was finished with me.

"Duneq said I could trust both of you to do exactly what I say, when I say it," Gaba said, after a final inspection of my helmet. "My boys will do the hard stuff." He pointed at the three men, now identical in black tactical gear, with masks pulled up to their goggles. "But you'll be close – closer than the local police. I want you ready to move in fast when I give the word." He reached out to unclip the radio on my shoulder, adjusting it so that it sat snugly on top of my vest.

I caught Atii's eye, followed by a flash of something that I hadn't seen before, as if she thought Gaba had paid me a little more attention than he should have. It might have been inappropriate, but it was enough to distract me from worrying about what was about to happen. But no matter what that look might have meant, it was neither the time nor the place to do anything about it. A shout from the wheelhouse confirmed it.

"He's running, Gaba," the skipper said, as he leaned out of the wheelhouse door to point at a small fibreglass dinghy punching through shallow waves away from the settlement.

"Still armed," said one of Gaba's men, as he lifted his goggles and pressed a pair of binoculars to his eyes.

"Skipper," Gaba shouted, clicking his fingers, and pointing to the shore. "Get the local police to come alongside in their boat. Atii," he said, snapping his head to one side to look at her. "As soon as they're here, you climb on-board and go back to Ingnerssuit. I want you to check on the women and children. Give your report to the skipper. Petra," he said, turning to me.

"Yes?"

"Grab one of the spare MP5s and put two extra magazines in the pouches on your vest."

"You're taking Petra with you?" Atii said, with another flash of jealousy in her eyes.

"Constable Napa," Gaba said, snapping his fingers as a small speedboat approached the cutter. "Your boat has arrived."

I tried to find something to say, but my tongue was dry again. And then it was too late, as Atii climbed over the railings and dropped down into the small rigid inflatable boat bumping against the side of the police cutter's hull.

"Ready, Constable?" Gaba said, tapping the front of my helmet with his knuckle.

I nodded, then lurched into Gaba's chest as the skipper pulled away from the smaller boat, opening up with the cutter's engine.

Part 2

I caught little more than a glimpse of Atii in the small dinghy sailing back to the settlement, before Gaba sent me to the wheelhouse with a curt nod of his shaved and oiled head. I stumbled over the lip of the door, grasped a handle to steady myself, and then found a spare MP5 submachine gun on a table beside the stairs leading below deck. I was familiar with the weapon, having trained with it at the Police Academy, but it felt cold and alien to my touch. I took another breath, focused on the submachine gun, the safety, the spare magazines. I opened the pouches at the front of my vest and tucked the magazines inside as Gaba spoke to the skipper.

"He's headed for Ivittuut," the skipper said. "Which is a problem."

"The abandoned mining town," Gaba said. "Why's that a problem?"

"Out of season, it's not. It's deserted. But if you look over there." The skipper took one hand off the wheel to point. "See the smokestack just above that berg?"

"I see it."

"That's the *MS Wisting*. A Norwegian adventure cruise ship. Eight decks. 280 Berths. About 400 passengers, plus crew."

"And they're visiting Ivittuut?"

"It's on the schedule." The skipper gripped the wheel and bent his knees in anticipation of a particularly large wave. "If we're lucky," he said, as I bumped into Gaba, recovering once *Sisak* had settled. "There's only one cruise ship. Otherwise…"

Gaba swore, then looked around the wheelhouse. He brushed past me and called down to the crew in the galley below deck.

"Do we have a rifle on board?"

"Like a hunting rifle?"

"*Aap*," Gaba said.

"Just a minute."

"What are you going to do?" I asked, as Gaba reached down the stairs to grab the barrel of an old bolt-action rifle, the kind the Sirius Sledge Patrol use to protect themselves from polar bears. Gaba ignored me as he worked the bolt and then reached down for a small magazine. "You're going to shoot him before he gets there, aren't you?"

Gaba said a curt thanks to the officer in the galley, and then strode across the wheelhouse to the door. He stuck his head into the wind, looked back at the rear deck and whistled.

"Taatsiaq," he said, thrusting the rifle into the arms of the first man to reach the wheelhouse. "You're the best shot with a rifle. Get up in the bow and prepare to take a shot."

Taatsiaq, a mini version of Gaba with thick black hair, lurched to one side as *Sisak* crested another wave. He gripped the rifle in one hand and the railing in the other as the cutter descended into the wave trough. "It's pretty rough, boss," he said.

"Tell me something I don't know." Gaba turned

back to the skipper. "How long before we reach Ivittuut?"

"Before we do, or before he does?"

"Us," Gaba said.

"Ten minutes."

"Okay, and him?"

"Six."

I watched Gaba as he sucked at his teeth, thinking. He glanced at the bow, watched Taatsiaq and another SRU team member use the railings to brace themselves against the motion of the boat. I saw Gaba nod to himself, as if the decision was made, which is when I made mine.

"You can't do it, Gaba," I said, stepping forward.

"That's not your decision, Constable."

"No? Then why did you bring me along?" I unclipped my helmet and held it under my arm, jerking the thumb of my free hand over my shoulder towards Ingnerssuit. "The women and children are back there."

"And there will be plenty more on that cruise ship," Gaba said. "I'm not going to let some old man with a gun put them in danger."

"His name is Eqqitsiaq Kuuania," I said. "He's a father, and a grandfather."

The skipper turned his head and I caught the look in his eye, warning me that I was treading dangerous waters. Sergeant Gaba Alatak was well known for his command decisions, his commitment to training, and his firm belief that in tactical situations, even when the commissioner was present, no one questioned his actions. Certainly not

13

a lowly police constable fresh out of the academy.

"Petra," he said. "This…"

"Isn't the time?" I almost laughed, as the butterflies in my stomach stopped flapping and I slapped the helmet down onto the table. "Atii says the nicest things about you," I said.

"You're out of line, Constable."

Gaba clenched his jaw and I saw his brown eyes darken as he narrowed his gaze, focusing on me, as if daring me to say one more thing. Which of course, I did, now that *training was over*. I'm sure that Sergeant Duneq would have put me in my place, perhaps even faster than Gaba was about to, but I wasn't going to stand by and let Taatsiaq, or anyone else, take pot shots at an old man fleeing from the police.

"She also says that she trusts you more than any other police officer, because you always make the right decision. Even when time is an issue."

"Time *is* an issue, Constable. I need to stop Kuuania before he puts people's lives at risk."

"He won't."

"You can't possibly know that."

"I know just as much as you," I said, surprising myself at the note of conviction in my voice. If I didn't know better, I'd say I was being influenced. How could I possibly know what Eqqitsiaq Kuuania, a man I had never met, would or wouldn't do? But something or *someone* was telling me to get involved, to risk everything, and, potentially, to risk the lives of 400 people from the cruise ship, should Eqqitsiaq run amok in Ivittuut. *That* was what Gaba wanted me to think of, and I did, as his words hung between us.

"You don't have the experience, Constable," he said, following up. "Don't make the mistake of pretending you know how this will end, because I guarantee you will be disappointed."

"And Eqqitsiaq will be dead. Is that it?"

"I didn't bring you onboard to…"

"What?" I said, stepping forward, closing the gap between us. "Tell me, Sergeant, why am I here?"

Gaba snorted. "I'm not playing that game."

"Then why I don't I tell you," I said, lowering my voice to a whisper. "Atii's the confident one. She's also better with a gun – *any* gun. She's the obvious choice. Except you brought me here to show off, and to piss her off. To make her jealous, that you picked me over her."

"You're out of line, Constable," Gaba said, leaning close.

"Am I? Then why are you whispering?"

The butterflies were back, and their crazy flight pattern sent a feathery burst of adrenaline through my body as I stared into Gaba's face, holding my ground, making a point, and, judging by the tic in his jaw, pissing him off entirely.

"How long, skipper?" he said, raising his voice while looking at me.

"He had to double back around some ice. We've closed the gap. He'll make land in maybe a minute or so. We're right behind him." The skipper coughed, waited for Gaba to turn, and then pointed at Taatsiaq in the bow. "Your boys are waiting for orders."

"Wave them in," Gaba said, turning back to me. "I want them here when I brief our new negotiator."

Part 3

As soon as we landed, no more than five minutes after Gaba's no-nonsense authoritarian brief on what he *did* and *did not* expect me to do or say, I felt the SRU leader's firm grip on my shoulder.

"I'll be right behind you," he said, his voice low, his pitch measured, and his meaning one hundred percent clear. "If I tell you to drop…"

"I drop," I said, knowing that I would.

"Then we have an understanding?"

"Yes."

"And," he said, with a nod to the police cutter moored next to Eqqitsiaq's dinghy at the dock behind us. "What you said, back on the boat, about Atii…"

At any other time, I might have found it irritating, or at least curious, that Gaba, or any man for that matter, might suddenly feel self-conscious about his actions. Instead, faced with talking a confused fugitive into giving himself up without a fight, Gaba's reaction to be called out served a different purpose, one I chose not to credit him with. In that moment, I forgot about Eqqitsiaq, for about two seconds, as I considered what to do with Sergeant Gaba Alatak.

Those few seconds were enough.

"It stays on the boat," I said. Followed by, "I'm

ready."

"I know you are," he said, as he reached out to adjust my vest one last time. Gaba shifted his grip on his MP5 submachine gun, then nodded to his team to enter Ivittuut.

The few tourists shuffling about the abandoned mining village stopped in their tracks as we entered the village. The skipper had called the captain on the *MS Wisting*, alerting him to the situation. Gaba's men directed the remaining tourists quietly but firmly back to the Zodiac rigid inflatable boats beached on the rough strip of gravel and sand just beyond the buildings. I heard a mix of broken English, German, and Danish words, as the SRU team cleared the village. A woman, dressed like a tour guide with a big radio in her small hands, pointed to a blistered house with a rotten deck and tiny squared windows, typically colonial, bitten by the wind, burned by the sun, and splintered by winter.

"He's in there," she said, then pointed with the tip of the radio's antenna. "I saw him go in."

I dipped my head in acknowledgement, then felt Gaba's hand on my shoulder, guiding me towards the house, while the three SRU men found sheltered positions covering the house and its exits. The guide jogged back to the Zodiacs on the beach.

"Put your helmet on, Constable," Gaba whispered.

"No," I said. "I don't want to frighten him."

"And I don't want to shoot him. But I will if he so much as farts in your direction. If you're wearing your helmet, I'll give him a second's worth of goodwill. Understand?"

"Yes," I said, as I unclipped my helmet from my belt and pulled it onto my head. Loose strands of my hair caught in the clip and I tugged them free. I didn't realise I was holding my breath until Gaba squeezed my arm.

"Whenever you're ready," he said.

Friday nights in Nuuk were often physical. Even the most patient and sympathetic police officer struggled with drunks too far gone to be reasonable. We trained for it, learned how to anticipate violence, to counter it, and put an end to it as quickly and respectfully as the situation allowed.

This was different.

Eqqitsiaq was armed, and he was clearly struggling with something, yet unknown. I knew little more than his name, and the fact that just a short boat ride earlier, he had laid siege to his own house, trapping his wife, his daughter, and his grandchildren inside. I had no idea what might make him do that, but the only way I would find out was if he was ready to talk.

I took a step forward, stopping when Gaba hissed that I shouldn't go too far. I heard him squirm his boots into a firm stance in the gravel outside the house, pictured him tugging the MP5 into his shoulder, using the sling to offset the weight of the weapon in anticipation of a lengthy *ready* stance. He clicked his tongue and I took that as my cue.

"Eqqitsiaq Kuannia," I said, clearing my throat before I continued. "My name is Constable Petra

Jensen. I'm here to help you."

It occurred to me, as the wind dusted spores of grit and ancient husks of cotton across my boots, that I didn't know if Eqqitsiaq could speak Danish. I suppressed a sudden thought that Atii would have been so much better at this than me, and another when I imagined Sergeant Duneq nodding his head in agreement. But Duneq had sent both Atii and me, and that gave me some hope that my presence had some purpose, beyond the egotistical and chauvinistic afflictions of the SRU leader.

"Again," Gaba whispered.

I took a small step forward, waving my hand for Gaba to relax, as I heard his sharp intake of breath. I was close to the deck now, close enough to see the rotten fibres of wood, twisting around rusty nails with long thatched fingers.

"Eqqitsiaq?"

I took another step, ignoring Gaba's curses, and the metallic clicks of the SRU team as they adjusted their aim. I lifted one foot onto the first step, testing it, pressing my boot down until I heard the wood tear with soft snaps and hushed crackles.

"My name is Constable Jensen," I said, climbing to the second step and reaching out for the winter-bitten wood railing. I pressed my fingers around it, felt it wobble in my grasp, then climbed the last step to the deck.

"Petra," Gaba said. "No further."

I stopped, nodded once, then leaned to one side to peer in through the open door. The wind wrenched it open with a squeal and a thud, enough to mask the sound of Eqqitsiaq's footsteps as he approached the door. I saw the barrel of his rifle first, as he pressed it against the door, pushing it slowly to open it wide, triggering my eyes to do the same.

"Eqqitsiaq," I whispered, as I watched his finger slide through the trigger guard of his rifle. "Don't."

Part 4

Eqqitsiaq Kuannia wore the wrinkles of long summer days with the hues of long dark winters. His cheeks were stubbled with black and grey hairs, with more grey in the thick hair on his head. His look matched his situation – tense, like his finger around the trigger, but his eyes held a sadness that threatened to bring a lump to my throat, if only it wasn't for the rifle pointed at my chest.

"Eqqitsiaq," I said, softly, drawing his attention to my face as I heard Gaba crunch through the gravel behind me. "Do you speak Danish?"

"*Aap*," he said. He tilted his head to one side, following Gaba's movements with the same sad eyes, now flecked with suspicion.

"That's Sergeant Alatak," I said. "We're both here to help you."

"He has a gun."

"Yes," I said, and then, "So do you."

Eqqitsiaq flicked his gaze back to me and I cursed, silently, as I thought about what I had said. I needed to speak *smarter*, although the very idea and phrasing of it almost made me laugh. I needed to get it together but standing between two men with guns didn't help.

"Can I come inside?"

"Not a good idea, Constable," Gaba said. "Stay

where you are."

I caught the flick of irritation on Eqqitsiaq's face, as if Gaba was intruding suddenly. He slapped the barrel of his rifle against the door as it started to creak open, then pushed it to one side as he beckoned for me to come with his free hand.

I flashed a look at Gaba, willing him to back off, as I unclipped my helmet and placed it on a rickety table sinking slowly into the soft wood of the deck.

"Thank you," I said, as I stepped inside the house. Eqqitsiaq backed away from the door, letting it close behind him as we entered the kitchen.

The interior of the house was bruised with age and the recent footsteps of curious tourists. I remembered that the mine was abandoned in 1987, but that the Danes had dug cryolite out of the earth for over one hundred years. Apart from the soft tread of Eqqitsiaq's tattered sneakers and the sturdy impressions of the tourists' boots, the dust on the floor revealed little more than whispers of ghosts. At least, that was what I felt as I sat down on one of two chairs still in one piece. Ghosts were a part of Greenlandic culture, everyone believed in them, including me. I shivered as Eqqitsiaq sat down. He slid the rifle onto the table between us, and I resisted the urge to grab it.

"You said you were shopping," he said, picking at an oily thread on the hem of his fleece. "But where is your bag?"

"What's that?" I said. "Shopping?"

"I waited. Your mother waited. She said you had been gone too long, I said we should wait.

There was plenty of coffee. We only needed sugar. But…" Eqqitsiaq's gaze drifted to my face, and he frowned. "You're not Ansu."

"No," I said.

Eqqitsiaq turned to look over his shoulder. "Where is Ansu?"

"She's not here. She's waiting in Ingnerssuit."

I reached for the rifle as Eqqitsiaq twisted in his chair to look through the tiny squares of the broken window.

"She said she would come straight home," he said.

"Yes."

I curled my fingers around the barrel of the rifle, sliding it towards me as Eqqitsiaq turned around. He flicked his head up, stared at me, then reached a wrinkled and scarred hand towards the rifle. He grabbed the stock just as I pulled it out of his grasp. Eqqitsiaq's knuckles rapped on the table surface, bouncing old dust and memories into the mouldy air between us.

"That's mine," he said, rising and heaving the table to one side.

I stood, stumbling backwards with the rifle in my hand, pulling it out of Eqqitsiaq's reach as he lurched towards me. The kitchen floor was as rotten as the deck outside, and I plunged my right foot through it, pinning my ankle and toppling onto the floor, crying out in surprise and then pain as I twisted under Eqqitsiaq's body. He gripped the rifle, ripping it from my hands just as Gaba burst through the door.

I held my breath. I almost closed my eyes,

anticipating the short burst of thunder and bullets that Gaba would unleash as he blasted Eqqitsiaq with his MP5. But Gaba didn't fire. Instead, he charged over my body, letting his MP5 swing free on its sling as he curled his fingers into the loose material of Eqqitsiaq's fleece, flinging the older Greenlander across the room. Gaba stooped to pick up Eqqitsiaq's rifle, clearing the bullet from the chamber and jettisoning the rest with fluid movements of the bolt. He emptied the rifle as his team entered the house, slapping it into the nearest man's hands before he knelt beside Eqqitsiaq, offering the old man his hand, then pulling him slowly, gently, into a sitting position.

"He's confused, Gaba," I said, as I worked my foot out of the rotten floorboards.

"About what?"

"Not *about* anything. He thought I was Ansu."

Eqqitsiaq looked at me as I said the name, and I caught a look of panic in his eye.

"My daughter," he said. "Iikkila will be worried."

"Yes," I said. I reached up to take Taatsiaq's hand as he pulled me onto my feet. "We can take you to Iikkila. If you're ready to come with us?"

Eqqitsiaq shrank to the kitchen wall, splaying his hands in the dust, leaving tracks like raven feathers in the snow. It made me think of Tuukula, the shaman, and how nothing is as it seems, and everything is as simple or as complicated as you want it to be.

"Eqqitsiaq," I said. "We're here to help you."

"I want to see Iikkila."

"Yes. And we can take you to her."

Gaba reached out, offering his hand, holding it steady until Eqqitsiaq took it.

"Come on," he said. "Let's take you home."

Part 5

Home was eerily quiet. The residents of Ingnerssuit watched without a word as we walked between the houses with Eqqitsiaq, Gaba leading, with one of his men either side of the old man. Taatsiaq tied Eqqitsiaq's dinghy to a thick link of iron chain attached to the rock, as I jogged along the beach to catch up with the four men. Eqqitsiaq had been slow and silent on board *Sisak III*, receiving sweet coffee with little more than raised eyebrows. But as soon as we arrived in Ingnerssuit, he became animated, bounding off the cutter towards his house with the SRU in tow.

Eqqitsiaq's grandchildren greeted him with cautious smiles as he climbed the steps onto the wooden deck outside his house. A plump woman waited for him, arms folded across her chest.

"Iikkila," Eqqitsiaq said, but she shook her head, shooing her husband away until Atii stepped between them.

"She's worried," Atii said, as Gaba helped Eqqitsiaq into a chair. "She wants us to take him to Nuuk."

"I can't arrest him for running away," Gaba said, pressing his hand onto Eqqitsiaq's shoulder, clamping him into his seat. "No one got hurt. This is a domestic disturbance at best."

Atii shook her head. "It's more than that. He's sick. Iikkila says he's confused. But," she said, lowering her voice, "he's not the only one."

"Explain," Gaba said. He nodded for one of his men to keep an eye on Eqqitsiaq, then pointed at a patch of tough straw-coloured grass a few metres from the house. I followed him and Atii off the deck, glancing once at Eqqitsiaq before Atii started to speak.

"Something's not right," she said, throwing me a look that suggested she was still pissed that Gaba had taken me instead of her, but that there were more pressing concerns. "The kids are a little high without being *high*, if you know what I mean?"

"Not in the slightest," Gaba said. "But you've been here the longest. What's your recommendation?"

"My recommendation?" Atii frowned.

"What do you suggest we do, Constable Napa?" Gaba hooked his thumbs into his utility belt. "I'm deferring to your judgement."

It could have been a peace offering, or perhaps it was Gaba showing a side of him neither of us had seen before, but it had Atii stumped, and I relaxed a little, eager to help my friend assume the responsibility that had just been given to her.

"If you think we should take Eqqitsiaq to hospital…"

"I don't know," she said, teasing her hand through her dark bobbed hair. "I think we should take all of them."

"All of them?" Gaba snorted. "Well, we can't do that."

"Eqqitsiaq then," Atii said. "Let's get him checked out. I'll tell his wife."

Atii turned away before I could say anything, leaving Gaba and I alone on the grass outside Eqqitsiaq's house.

"Sergeant," I said, once Atii was out of earshot.

"*Aap*?"

"Don't do that to me again. Don't do it to either of us."

"Don't do what?"

"Choose me over her, to send a message."

"I wasn't sending a *message*, Constable."

"No?" I took a breath, glancing at Atii where she waited, watching us from the deck of Eqqitsiaq's house. "Whatever you were doing, whatever you were trying to prove, next time you have to choose someone, I suggest you choose the one best suited for the job." I turned on my heel and walked away, barely catching Gaba's words on the wind.

"I thought I did," he said.

I walked back to the police cutter, leaving Gaba and Atii to organise Eqqitsiaq's departure. I sat on a rock on the beach, looking out at the red-hulled police cutter loitering just off the shore. Taatsiaq waved from the inflatable as he powered back towards the beach. *It would take two trips*, I thought, idly running through the practical details of getting us all back on board *Sisak III*, the last decisions I thought I would make in the case of Eqqitsiaq Kuannia.

Of course, Tuukula had other plans.

Part 6

The nightclub was Gaba's idea, a chance to blow off steam and regroup after the trip to Ingnerssuit. Atii had balked at the suggestion, but I saw a chance to be the friend I knew I was, and to remind her that a man was never going to come between us, never split us apart. Once Eqqitsiaq was admitted to hospital, I convinced her to come to *Mattak*, agreeing that I would meet her there, and that, if she didn't come, I would leave. Whatever Gaba was, however curious I might have been to get to know him, it was Atii who was interested in him, and me... well, I was normally the naive type, and I could easily be that for one more night.

Clubbing in Nuuk had to account for the weather, and even in May it could be cold, often wet, with stubborn patches of ice clumping the gravel on the unfinished sides of the streets. I settled on skinny jeans and a checked blouse. But when I saw Atii my breath caught in my throat. Her bobbed hair was fixed with spray at the back as if she was speeding on a motorbike with no helmet. Her eyes sparkled, with just enough eyeliner to give her a killer stare. Together with the skin-tight tank top and equally tight black leather trousers, I knew Gaba was the least of my problems. If *I* couldn't take my eyes off Atii, then neither would he. And he didn't, the whole night. At least, not until Tuukula arrived.

We had a booth tucked along one wall of the club, something Taatsiaq had arranged with his brother, the current owner of *Mattak*. The square dance floor writhed with gymnasium students aged seventeen and up, sometimes younger, together with men and women in their twenties and thirties. I smiled at the thought that Gaba was one of the oldest in the club. But he wore his age like a badge of honour, earned through experience. His usual persona, however, was knocked out of kilter by Atii's outfit, and the need to win back her affections.

I left them to it when Taatsiaq invited me onto the dance floor. He took my hand and tugged me deep into the throng of bodies until the booth was gone and there was only the beat, phasing stutters of music, strobes and zigzags of purple and pink light. Taatsiaq pressed his left hand on my waist, his right testing and teasing, slipping over my hips, curving around my bottom. I paused for a moment, curious as to how far I would let him go, how far I *wanted* him to go. I brushed a length of hair out of my face, behind my ear. I felt sweat bead on my top lip, felt it under my arms, running down my ribs in hot streams. My shirt was too thick for the dance floor. I swallowed, felt the brush of a woman's skin on my bare arm as she danced in her bra, and I thought about doing the same, if only for a second, before Taatsiaq moved in closer, pressing against me, until his lips were close to mine, closer than I imagined they would ever have been just a few hours earlier.

But if I wanted to prove to Atii that I would never come between her and Gaba, wasn't this the most perfect situation? Showing her that we were friends, that we would have plenty to talk about, to giggle about over coffee, or sprawl on the sofa, whispering gossip after a late-night shift. I let Taatsiaq move in closer, pressed my lips against his, felt the heat of him, felt his excitement grow in the press of his body, the grip of his fingers, until shouts and the smash of glasses on the floor turned our heads, as the dancers parted. Tuukula stood in the gap with his daughter Luui clutched to his side, ringed by irritated dancers, and the barman doing his best to order the old shaman to leave.

"Petra," Tuukula said, ignoring everyone around him. "I need to talk."

"You know him?" Taatsiaq said, with a jerk of his thumb.

"Yes," I said.

I plucked at my shirt, suddenly conscious of my damp armpits, the sweat blistering strands of my hair to my forehead, and the tumult of confused endorphins stirred by Taatsiaq's intentions, only to be quashed by the arrival of a seventy-year-old man and his five-year-old daughter.

"I have to go," I said. "Thanks for the dance."

"He can't bring the girl in here," the barman said, as I stepped off the dance floor.

"It's all right. We're leaving," I said, as Luui lurched out of Tuukula's arms and into mine. She nuzzled her face into my neck, then pulled back to wipe her nose, whispering something to her father in Greenlandic.

"She says you're all sweaty," Tuukula said.

"She's right." I flicked my finger towards the booth along the wall and started walking towards it, skirting around the dance floor. "I need my jacket."

"I've been dumped for an older guy," Taatsiaq said as he slid into the booth beside Gaba. He reached for his glass, lifted it in a mock toast, then drained the last slug of beer as I tugged my jacket out from behind Atii's back.

"Sorry," I said. "Maybe another time?"

"Maybe," Taatsiaq said.

I reached out for Atii's hand, holding her fingers as I said, "You're beautiful, Atii."

Atii smiled, then squeezed my hand and I felt a flood of warmth course through my body – forgiven, for the moment.

"Petra," Tuukula said softly, as he approached the booth. "We have to go."

Part 7

"We'll need a taxi," I said, pressing Luui into Tuukula's arms as I put on my jacket. I was still waiting for some kick of irritation, or the pinch of skin above my nose – just beneath my frown of curiosity, but what I felt most was relief. Not because Taatsiaq was not my type, only that I didn't have a type. I wasn't looking. I went to *Mattak* for Atii's sake, and once her situation was resolved – or on the mend, at least – my sense of responsibility evaporated, just like the glimpse of passion on the dance floor when Tuukula gate-crashed the nightclub.

"Just how did you get Luui past the bouncers at the door?" I asked, as Tuukula waved for a taxi driver to pick us up in the line outside Hotel Hans Egede.

"I said I needed to see you and they let me in."

"They're not supposed to."

"They didn't seem concerned."

"You mean you tricked them?"

Tuukula shrugged as the taxi pulled alongside us. "I said nothing they didn't agree with."

"*Ataata* used magic," Luui said, as she tumbled out of Tuukula's arms and onto the back seat.

"Only a little," he said, as he got in beside her.

The taxi driver chatted all the way to my

apartment in Qinngorput. Luui scrambled over her father's legs, squeezing between us, and plucking at my fingers as we drove. I felt the soft stab of her thumbs in my thighs as I tugged my purse out of my jacket pocket. Tuukula and Luui waited outside the entrance to the apartment block as I paid, following me inside as soon as the taxi pulled away. I could see Tuukula wanted to talk by the way he fidgeted, something I didn't remember ever seeing him do before.

"We'll take the lift," I said, telling Luui which button to press, before leaning against the polished railing.

Tuukula said nothing before we entered my apartment, letting Luui do the talking for him, as the details of their journey south from Qaanaaq bubbled out of her in a mix of Greenlandic and Danish, spiced with a few words in English.

"It's late," I said, as I hung my jacket by the door. "I guess you'll stay the night?"

"*Aap*," Tuukula said. He pulled a toothbrush out of his pocket and pressed it into Luui's hand, nodding at the bathroom and encouraging her with a soft pat on her bottom. He waited until Luui turned on the water, and then said, "It's about a friend of mine."

"Who?"

"Eqqitsiaq Kuannia. He needs our help."

"Eqqitsiaq? The man from Ingnerssuit? Why?"

Tuukula said nothing more until Luui had snuggled beneath the covers of my spare bed. She wriggled from one side to the other as Tuukula tried to tuck her in, then held out her hands, drawing me into the room at the end of an imaginary rope she heaved on with exaggerated tugs and wheezes.

"Goodnight, Luui," I said, kissing her freckled nose.

"Goodnight, pretty woman," she said, and giggled.

"You think so?"

"*Aap.*"

"All right then," I said. "Sleep now."

I turned out the light on my way out of the room, leaving the door ajar when Luui protested at me closing it.

"Go to sleep, Luui," Tuukula said.

I stifled a yawn as I checked my smartphone, wondering where Atii was, and how fit we would be for work the next day. "Later today," I whispered to myself, before joining Tuukula in my kitchen.

"I don't have any tea," I said. "Just coffee."

"Coffee is fine."

Tuukula sat straight and tall on the chair, resting his arms on the table in front of him, lacing his fingers tight as he watched me. I had never seen him so quiet, so concerned.

"We took Eqqitsiaq to the hospital today," I said.

"I know."

"And before that…"

"You chased him to Ivittuut." Tuukula nodded his head, slowly. "I know that too."

"How? Were you already in Nuuk?"

"I arrived this evening – late. I came straight from the airport to the nightclub."

"How did you know I was there?"

Tuukula shrugged. "It's not important."

A flat smile crept onto my lips as I recognised Tuukula's simple evasion. Tuukula's *magic*, as Luui called it, wasn't something he tried to hide, but neither did he feel the need to explain it at length, at least no more than was necessary. I placed a mug of coffee in front of him and sat down at the table, blowing on my own drink as I waited for him to speak.

"Eqqitsiaq is my friend," he said. "And he needs our help."

"How?"

"You met him today."

"Yes."

Tuukula nodded. "I wanted to visit him at the hospital, but they said he was sleeping. I think he was sedated." He paused to take a sip of coffee. "Was he confused?"

"Very. He thought I was his daughter."

"When?"

"In the house, in Ivittuut."

"You followed him inside?"

"Yes," I said. "I took his gun."

Tuukula sighed, and said, "Eqqitsiaq is not himself. You could have been hurt."

"Actually, I think he just needed to talk."

"And you talked to him? What did he say?"

"Not much." I put my mug down and warmed my hands around it. "Gaba came in shortly after I took Eqqitsiaq's rifle. I thought it was all over, until you showed up."

"I had to come," Tuukula said.

"Because he's your friend?"

"Because he's in trouble. They all are. Everyone in Ingnerssuit."

Part 8

I lit a candle, curious at the way the light flickered in Tuukula's eyes, teasing shadows out of his grey hair, the tuft on top of his head, and casting them onto the wall behind him. I sipped at my coffee as he talked, describing a younger Tuukula, many years before Luui and I were born, when he and Eqqitsiaq worked the cryolite mine in Ivittuut.

"It used to be just Danes, Canadians and Americans working at the mine," he said. "Although, there were some Greenlanders working in the kitchen. Then, in the 80s, before the mined closed, there were a few Greenlanders working inside the mine. Just a handful."

"Including you and Eqqitsiaq."

"*Aap.*" Tuukula paused for a smile and a sip of coffee. "It was hard work, lots of machinery, lots of history, too. We told stories in the evenings, some of them about the war."

"What war?"

"The Second World War," he said. "Before your time, and just before mine. Denmark was occupied. But not Greenland. The Americans were here, protecting the mine with their soldiers. They needed the cryolite to refine aluminium for planes."

"I didn't know," I said.

Tuukula shrugged. "Not many people do. We

don't talk about the war in Greenland like they do in Europe. But the mine carried on long after the war, closing down in 1987. I was thirty-nine. Eqqitsiaq was a year younger. He met Iikkila. She worked in the kitchen." Tuukula grinned and cupped his hands to his chest. "She had big breasts, and Eqqitsiaq couldn't take his eyes off them." Tuukula chuckled and reached for his coffee. He took a sip, wiped his mouth with the back of his hand, then patted the side of his head, fiddling with his ear, as if searching for the cigarette he often kept there. "I must have smoked them already," he said. "Anyway, Iikkila told my friend that if he was going to spend so much time looking at her breasts, then he should be useful while he did it. She had him carrying all the heavy things from the boat to the pantry each time the kitchen was resupplied. This was in his free time, when he was finished in the mine for the day."

"And they got married," I said.

"*Aap*. She married Eqqitsiaq. He did whatever she told him to do. And they moved to Ingnerssuit, where her family came from, the place where she was born."

I thought about the Eqqitsiaq I had met, the wild glint in his eyes, as if he was unmoored, adrift without direction.

"What happened to him?"

"I don't know." Tuukula turned the mug in his hands, distracted by the last dregs of coffee as they swirled around the bottom of the mug. "We lost touch. I found a job on a fishing trawler out of Ilulissat. He stayed in the south. I never saw him again. But last month, Iikkila called me. She said Eqqitsiaq was sick, and that he wasn't the only one. She knew about me. I think Eqqitsiaq told her once about my father, how he was *angakkoq*, how medicine ran in our family, and how I was chosen to be a shaman by my father. She thought I could heal Eqqitsiaq. She still thinks I can heal him."

"Can you?"

Tuukula looked up, a fierce light burning in his eyes, only to flicker and die before me. "Petra," he said. "You know that's not how it works."

"Then she wants you to help in some other way," I said, clutching at straws in the face of Tuukula's uncharacteristic sadness. "There must be something you can do. That's why Iikkila called you."

"There is something I can do. But I can't do it alone. I will need your help."

Part 9

"Forget about it, Jensen." Sergeant Duneq's jowls wobbled as he shook his head. "You're working the next four weekends, starting tomorrow. Even if you had leave, which you don't, you still couldn't go."

"Why not?" I asked, conscious that Tuukula and Luui were having breakfast in *Katuaq*, and that I had promised to join them as soon as I had talked with my supervisor. "I'm following up on a case."

"A case?" Duneq laughed. "You are a constable, Jensen. You're not a detective. You don't work *cases*. And no," he said, waving a fat finger in front of me. "The Missing Persons desk doesn't count. And, even if it did. There's no one missing, *Constable*. Kuannia is in Dronning Ingrid's Hospital. You took him there. The rest of the family is in Ingnerssuit. No one is *missing*, Jensen. You can't go swanning off on your own assignment this time." Duneq snorted, then wiped his nose with his thumb. "You're stuck, with me, here in Nuuk. Get used to it."

"But the Commissioner…"

"Constable Jensen," Duneq said. The desk between us shook as he slapped his palms on the surface. "The Commissioner can't help you, even with those favours you do for him. That's right," he said, sneering as he spoke. "You thought I didn't know about your little editing sessions. It's funny, for a *girl* of your supposed intellect, you're not very clever after all, are you?"

"I just…"

"What?"

"It's Tuukula. He's helped me before."

"Right, your *angakkoq* – the magician. Is that him? Gaba told me all about how he brought that little girl to the nightclub."

"Luui is his daughter. He couldn't leave her alone."

I felt my cheeks flush, a sure sign I should have stopped long before I reached this point. But I was desperate now and failed to recognise the warning looks flashed by my colleagues sitting close by at their desks in the open office area.

"Luui?"

"Yes," I said. "She's five."

"Your shaman friend brought a five-year-old to a nightclub?"

"Yes," I said, weaker now, less convinced.

Duneq shook his head, and said, "I rest my case. You have no case. This conversation is over. Perhaps you should get some rest? I don't recommend that my officers go clubbing midweek, especially not when they have an evening shift the following day. Perhaps that explains your total lack of judgement." Duneq cocked his head to one side, baiting or waiting for me to speak.

"I just…"

"Yes?"

"Nothing," I said, after catching another warning glance from the officer seated at the desk closest to Duneq's. "There's no case."

"There isn't."

"I don't work cases."

"That's right, Constable. You don't."

"I'll be back later, for my shift."

"That's exactly what you are going to do, Jensen."

Duneq's chair creaked as he sat down. I paused for a second, glancing at my own desk and the broken chair tucked beneath it at the far end of the room. If the phone rang, I was allowed to answer it, as per the Commissioner's instructions. But if it didn't ring, there was no case. And if no one was missing, there was nothing to be done. Tuukula was alone on this one.

"Maybe I didn't explain it properly," Tuukula said, as I sat down between him and Luui at their table in *Katuaq*. "I was tired. I should have told you."

"Told me what?"

"That someone *is* missing."

"From Ingnerssuit?"

"*Aap.*"

I glanced at Luui as she patted my arm with her tiny hand. She had such big brown eyes; one could get lost in them.

"I don't understand," I said, turning my head from Luui to look at her father. "Unless someone is reported missing, they have probably just moved away."

"*Naamik,*" Tuukula said, with a shake of his head. "This man is not missing. He just disappeared."

"Who?"

"The one Iikkila said has all the answers."

"Do you know his name?"

"Why?"

"Because if you called this number," I said, writing the extension of the number for the phone on my desk on a napkin, "you could report him missing."

"I'm telling you he is."

"Yes," I said. "But that's not how it works. At least, not for me. You have to call this number. You have to report him missing. And then I can help you."

Tuukula frowned, and said, "It seems like a complicated way to ask for police assistance."

"You have no idea," I said, with a sigh. "But, if you call I can help."

"*Poof*," Luui said, as she splayed her fingers. "Like magic."

"Yes," I said. "Something like that."

Part 10

Police Commissioner Lars Andersen was new to Greenland but not to policing. He understood the bigger picture that stretched further, beyond Sergeant Duneq's sphere of influence, digging deeper into the community, its roots and culture. Danish or Greenlandic, the principles were the same and the commissioner applied them. It was his opinion that the missing persons desk fulfilled a role for the wider community, a role that might sometimes be hard to define when a missing person becomes just another investigation alongside regular police work. Having a dedicated number to call provided community members with the means of differentiating between someone who was lost, requiring immediate help, or someone who had been missing for a longer period. Sometimes the lines were blurred. Sometimes the missing persons simply didn't want to be found, often turning up in Denmark years later. But each case presented some form of closure, for better or worse. As I understood it, it was the *closure* that interested the commissioner most, identifying the need and applying the necessary tools and people to achieve it. Which is why it was fortunate he was in the office at the start of my shift when Duneq answered the phone on my desk.

I had never seen Duneq so quiet, nor so flushed as he listened to the caller provide the details, circumstances, and description of the missing person. Duneq reached for the notepad on my desk, flipped it open to a new page, and started making notes as he spoke, clarifying the details.

"In his seventies? Medium height. Slight build. Grey hair, often worn bunched at the top of his head?"

I bit my lower lip, turning away from Duneq and the commissioner as I realised the caller, who I knew to be Tuukula, was describing himself. I swallowed as Duneq ended the call and turned to the commissioner with his notes.

"Honestly, I don't know what to make of it," he said. "The caller…" Duneq paused as he searched his notes for a name. "Isak Petrussen, claims that an older man, also Petrussen – may be a relative, with the first name Ivan." Duneq snorted, snapping the notepad closed as he leaned against the edge of my desk. "Apparently Ivan went missing over a year ago."

"From where?" the commissioner asked.

I knew where. I dipped my head as Duneq stared at me for a second, before answering the commissioner's question.

"Ingnerssuit," he said. "It's same settlement where Eqqitsiaq Kuannia was living."

"Kuannia? The man Gaba brought in?"

"Together with Constables Jensen and Napa," Duneq said.

"A coincidence," the commissioner said.

"*Aap*," Duneq said, casting another long look at

me.

"Well," the commissioner said. "You know my policy on this. As long as we have the budget for it, and if you can free Constable Jensen from her current duties, I think we should investigate."

"It will mean overtime for the officers replacing her," Duneq said. "I'm not sure it's worth the…"

"Time or money, Sergeant? This won't be the first time we dip into overtime. Put Constable Jensen on a plane or a boat, whatever is available. Give her three days and we'll see what comes of it. Does that sound like a plan?"

Duneq nodded, and, with little more than a grunt of confirmation, he pushed away from the desk. The commissioner caught my arm as I turned to leave.

"Just a minute, Constable," he said, with a nod to Duneq as he walked to his desk at the other end of the open office.

"Yes, Sir?" I said.

"That description of the missing man…"

"Yes?"

I caught a flash of something in the commissioner's eyes that could have been a warning. I swallowed and waited for him to continue.

"The description fits that of an older man who brought a young girl to a nightclub the other night. That same description was given by the bouncers at the door, as they tried to explain why they had let him in in the first instance. Have you seen that report, Constable?"

"No, Sir."

"Well, when you get a chance," the commissioner said, letting go of my arm. "You might find it interesting. Especially the part where the bouncers describe being confused, that the man – the one with the tuft of hair on top of his head – confused them into letting him into the nightclub."

"He confused them?"

"It's unclear how. But it reminded me of the article about you in *Suluk*. It was very entertaining, if a little sensational. There was something about a shaman?"

"Yes, Sir."

The glint in the commissioner's eyes was gone, replaced with a faint smile on his lips. But his manner suggested that I should prepare myself for a reprimand of sorts. I just didn't know what kind.

"Let's agree on this, Constable. I've given you a lot of leniency and very little oversight when it comes to these missing persons cases."

"It was your…"

"Yes," he said, cutting me off with a wave of his hand. "I asked you to answer the telephone that day. I gave you this responsibility, and you have had some results already. But let me be clear, you mustn't abuse the position, Constable. I don't doubt that you are working on a case. And I recognise the assistance your shaman…"

"Tuukula, Sir."

The commissioner nodded. "I understand that he has been of service and has helped in a number of cases so far. But this is the first and last time I make any exceptions for you. I need Sergeant Duneq's loyalty… Don't laugh, Constable. I know how he treats you. But one day you'll thank him. And one day you might even realise just how much he cares about you – professionally."

"He cares?"

"Of course, he does. Just don't expect him to show it. Now, go to Ingnerssuit. You have seventy-two hours." The commissioner reached around me to tear Duneq's notes from my pad. "You'll need these," he said, smiling as he turned away.

I waited until the commissioner had left the office, then stuffed the notes into my shirt pocket. Duneq glared at me as I walked past his desk, and I could feel his stare boring into my back as I walked out of the office, all the way to the station entrance. Tuukula and Luui were waiting outside.

"You gave a description of yourself," I said, quietly hurrying Tuukula away from the door. Luui slipped her hand in mine as we walked across the parking lot to the cultural centre.

"I thought that was quite clever," Tuukula said. "If your Sergeant Duneq measures these cases by success, then when you produce me as the missing person, you will be able to say the case is solved."

"The commissioner knows," I said, after a brief shake of my head.

"He's a smart man. They both are."

I stopped walking. That was the second time someone had praised Sergeant Duneq – twice within the same hour.

"Is there anything else?" I asked, as Luui tugged at my hand.

"*Aap*," Tuukula said, slipping a newly rolled cigarette behind his ear. "I have found us a boat.

We'll be sailing to Ingnerssuit."

"Great," I said, rolling my eyes at Luui as we remembered the last time we had been on a boat together. "Perfect."

Part 11

In a country with no connecting roads between towns and villages, boats of all sizes are essential. Nearly every family owns a boat, or has access to one, so it was no surprise that Tuukula knew someone in Nuuk from whom he could borrow a boat. I just wished it could have been bigger.

Luui snuggled between my legs, her head hidden deep inside the hood of her buoyancy-lined sea suit, as she picked at the buckles of mine. I kept my hood down, dipping my nose inside the stiff collar when it got too cold, letting my hair stream behind me in the wind. Tuukula smoked his two roll-up cigarettes, one straight after the other, one hand on the extended tiller, as he guided the long fibreglass dinghy between errant floes of ice south to Paamiut. He kept the bow relatively light, with just a few spare cans of fuel pressing it down towards the water. Luui and I rested on kitbags and assorted soft gear, trimming the boat, and leaving Tuukula in the stern. We dozed, he drove, waking us when he spotted whales, or when he needed to eat.

We had two coolers full of sandwiches, drinks, and dried strips of halibut that Tuukula would chew on, nibbling the white flesh and letting the skin slap against his cheeks before spitting it over the side of the boat and into the wind. I poured the coffee, reaching back to press a dirty plastic mug into Tuukula's hands, before wrinkling my nose at the fishy smell leaking out of the sides of my own mug each time I pressed it to my lips. Luui drank apple juice – more than Tuukula thought she should. He slowed the dinghy each time I tugged Luui out of her suit, holding her over the gunwales to pee.

"Not far now," Tuukula said, as we passed Paamiut. "Another sleep and we'll be there."

I nodded as I zipped Luui back into her suit, teasing her with eyelash kisses on her cheeks before she disappeared inside her hood. The water was calm, the sun high in the sky, and the wind was at our backs. I hoped the return journey would be just as smooth.

Tuukula drank the last of the coffee, then chewed the last strips of halibut as he steered the boat along the coast to the settlement of Ingnerssuit, calling out for us to wake as we approached. He cut the power, drifting the boat towards the beach, until the bow bumped gently onto the sand. I saw the spot where I had sat waiting for Gaba and Atii, before taking the painter from the bow to tie it to the links of rusted chain wrapped around a large boulder. Luui clambered over the gunwales, wobbling on her feet until she felt the familiar tug of the land and regained her balance.

Iikkila and her daughter walked down the beaten earth path to the beach to join us, hugging Tuukula then holding their arms wide to receive Luui as she ran towards them.

"I didn't think you would come so soon,"

Iikkila said, in Danish, most likely for my benefit.

"I've come to help," Tuukula said.

"Have you seen Eqqitsiaq?"

"He was sleeping. I didn't want to disturb him." Tuukula waved for me to come closer. "You remember Constable Jensen?"

"*Aap*," Iikkila said. "She took Eqqitsiaq to Nuuk."

"And now she's here to help."

Ansu laughed as Luui wrestled her way out of her sailing suit, calling to her own children to help. I watched as two boys took the legs of Luui's suit and pulled, bumping her bottom along the path as they dragged her towards the houses of Ingnerssuit. Luui giggled as they slid under a line of bright clothes hanging on the washing line, and then disappeared behind the houses and out of sight.

"I don't have much time," I said, unzipping my suit. "Perhaps, if I could ask some questions, we could get started?"

"This way," Iikkila said. "I have food ready."

Part 12

Tuukula said he would join us in a moment, leaving me with the two women as we walked between the red and blue houses. Iikkila chatted about Eqqitsiaq and Tuukula, how she could have married both of them, but of the two of them, Eqqitsiaq seemed like the least trouble. Ansu laughed when Iikkila pointed at Luui, now out of her suit, but clinging to it as the boys pulled her from one house to the next. Apart from the boys, Ingnerssuit seemed deserted, something I hadn't thought about before.

"Everyone who could leave has gone," Iikkila said.

"Why?"

Iikkila took her daughter's hand, as she laughed again, whispering to her, calming her until she stopped laughing, and then, with a heavy tread, Ansu climbed the steps to the deck and disappeared inside the house.

"She's struggling, now that Eqqitsiaq is in Nuuk."

"Struggling?"

I tried to remember what Atii had said, about the children being high. But watching the boys spin Luui between the houses, they seemed high-spirited, full of energy, but nothing out of the ordinary. Iikkila tapped my arm and pointed to a yellow house with a white deck. It was partly obscured by two other houses – Ingnerssuit had twelve houses in total – and I had to step to one side to see all of it.

"The school," Iikkila said. "Before the teacher left."

"When?"

"She left thirteen months ago."

Iikkila could have said *just over a year ago*, but she was more precise, as if it was important.

"And you haven't had a replacement?"

Iikkila shook her head and pointed at the boys. "I've been teaching them, as best I could. A lot of baking, sports. Some science when Eqqitsiaq caught a fish. But I don't know numbers, and I can't force them to speak Danish."

She paused as Tuukula strolled between the houses, puffing smoke around the cigarette clamped between his lips. His hands were full, gripping the handles of the holdalls and bags into which we had hastily stuffed clothes and bottled water – something Tuukula insisted on – before leaving Nuuk.

"Tuukula could teach them things," Iikkila said, pressing her hand to his cheek as he stopped beside her.

"I'm too old to teach children," he said.

"What about Luui?" Iikkila tucked her hands on her hips, knuckles inwards, slipping into imaginary grooves as if she did it often. "You're teaching her, aren't you?"

"That's different," Tuukula said, with a quick glance at his daughter. "They won't teach her what she needs to know in school."

"Iikkila says everyone is leaving," I said. "And the school has no teacher."

"We are nine," she said. "Ten if Eqqitsiaq was home." Iikkila slipped her hands from her hips, dusting the last flour from her palms with strong claps of her hands. "Let's go inside." She called for the two boys to come, then led the way up the steps to her house.

"Here," Tuukula said, pressing a bottle of water into my hands.

"I'm not thirsty," I said.

"For when you are."

"Tuukula?"

I waited for him to explain, but he shook his head, as if to say *not now*, and then followed Iikkila into the house. I kicked off my boots and shrugged out of my sailing suit, hanging it over the railing, before walking inside. Ansu and Tuukula were already sitting at the kitchen table, as Iikkila slid huge plates of raisin bread and strips of dried whale meat onto the table.

"You can eat the bread," Iikkila said. "I used a little water from the pan." She pointed at a large pan with a lump of melting ice on the counter as I sat down.

"I'm sure it's delicious," Tuukula said. "Iikkila made all the bread at the mine."

"You don't have water in the tank?" I asked, frowning as Iikkila swapped a glance with Tuukula.

"*Aap*," she said. "For washing only. Ever since we found out."

"Found out what?"

"That it was poisoned."

Iikkila reached out to take her daughter's hand as she started to laugh.

Part 13

I sat quietly as Ansu's laughter faded into a soft sobbing. She pushed back her chair and left the table. Iikkila followed her out of the kitchen, leaving Tuukula and I alone. I waited for him to say something, *anything*, prompting him with raised eyebrows and a nervous tap of my finger on the table.

"The commissioner knows it was you who called," I said. "I could get in a lot of trouble. Something is going on. I can see that. But you said someone is missing, but apart from people leaving Ingerssuit, I don't know who I'm supposed to be looking for."

"There is more to the story," he said.

"I'm sure there is, but unless you give me more information, there's nothing I can do, and you're just wasting police time."

Tuukula took a piece of raisin bread from the plate, then buttered it with slow strokes of a broad knife. He paid attention to the corners, spreading the butter to the very edges. It felt like he was drawing out the time, waiting for something. Then he called out in Greenlandic, and Iikkila returned with what looked like a large scrapbook in her hands. Tuukula cleared a spot on the table in front of me, then nodded at Iikkila to give me the book.

"The answers," he said, pointing with the tip of the butter knife, "are in there."

The pages crackled as I opened the book, stiff with glue, now dried in patches, barely holding clippings from newspapers and magazines. Most of the articles were in Danish, with a few translations in columns beside the main body of text.

"Pollution?" I said, looking up from the scrapbook.

"Keep reading," Tuukula said.

I checked the dates of each article. The earliest were dated four years back, with a few older magazine clippings with faded print. Most of the articles were written by the same man: Ivan Haarløv.

"Not Petrussen?" I said, tapping the journalist's name with the tip of my finger.

"I couldn't remember his name." Tuukula pulled out his tin of tobacco and rolled a cigarette. "He changes his name," he said. "He wrote those articles shortly after he came to Greenland."

"Four years ago."

"*Aap.*"

"He's Danish," I said, turning the page to skim read the next articles, columns, and opinion pieces. "He's an activist worried about pollution."

"About aluminium," Tuukula said. He tucked the finished cigarette behind his ear. "He was against the aluminium smelter, saying that it would cause significant pollution, dangerous to wildlife, the environment, and to people."

"But he lacked proof." I ran my finger beneath the lines of a paragraph that was repeated in three articles, notably from newspapers, and not written by Haarløv. "They said his allegations were baseless." I turned to the middle of the scrapbook, scanning the last clipping as Tuukula spoke.

"Or based on little evidence." Tuukula shrugged. "Haarløv needed proof."

"But this last article," I said, noting the date, "was two years ago."

"*Aap.*"

"So, he stopped writing?"

"Or he changed tactics."

"What does that mean?"

Tuukula turned to Iikkila. He took her hand as she sat down, squeezing it once, before nodding for her to speak. I got the impression that she was about to confess, as if she was guilty of something. I closed the scrapbook and waited for her to speak.

"We have a water tank and a pump," she said, drawing her hands into her lap. "The pump broke two years ago. Nukissiorfiit, the energy and water company, sent a man to fix it. He fixed the pump and went away again."

"Two years ago?" I said, as I opened my notebook. I paused to take a picture of Haarløv's photo with my phone.

"*Aap.* In April, I think." Iikkila licked her lips and Tuukula offered her water from one of the bottles he brought from the boat. "Everything was fine, but then, after half a year, I noticed Eqqitsiaq would forget things." Iikkila paused for a long, ragged breath. "At first, I teased him about it, told him he was getting old, that I would have to find a younger man. But then he forgot more and more things, like where he left his hammer, or how to tie his laces. I was worried, but Eqqitsiaq didn't want to go to the doctor. One day my neighbour said her mother was acting strangely. She thought she had dementia – she was forgetting things too. Acting confused. They took her to Paamiut to see a doctor. They never came back. They were the first to leave. Then the children started to have trouble breathing, like asthma. Ansu's children," she said, turning her head to look through the door into the living room.

Iikkila stopped talking and Tuukula took over, holding her hand as she lowered her head.

"They didn't know what was happening," he said. "They had no reason to think there was anything wrong."

"But these articles," I said, gesturing at the scrapbook. "Why did Iikkila start to collect them?"

"Because Ansu met the man, Haarløv, when she went to Nuuk for a language course. She recognised him."

"How?"

"Because he was the man Nukissiorfiit sent to fix the water pump," Iikkila said.

"She remembered him?"

Iikkila shrugged, and said, "We don't get many visitors. This man was Danish. He was handsome. Ansu remembered him."

"And she saw him in Nuuk?"

"He was a teacher at the gymnasium, where Ansu went for the course. She saw him in the corridor. He talked to her and asked her how things were in Ingnerssuit."

"And she told him," Tuukula said.

Iikkila nodded. "She told him her father was sick, and that her sons were suffering from asthma. She told him that people were leaving Ingnerssuit."

"And did he say anything?" I asked.

"Nothing," Iikkila said. "Or nothing that made any sense to Ansu. At least not then."

I turned my head as Ansu entered the kitchen. She stopped at the door, brushing at the tears on her cheeks with her fingers. She looked at her mother, then Tuukula, before turning to look at me.

"He asked me if we were leaving," she said. "I said no. I told him that we couldn't leave because we had no money, and that *ataata* was ill. I told him we would never leave."

"And what did he say?"

Ansu swallowed and took another look at her mother. "He said that was good."

Part 14

Tuukula slipped his tobacco tin into his trouser pocket, then nodded for me to follow him outside. We left the two women in the kitchen. Ansu's sobbing followed us out of the kitchen and onto the deck, until Tuukula closed the front door with a soft click. Tuukula spent a moment rooting through a box of Eqqitsiaq's tools, choosing a claw hammer as I tugged my boots on. I followed him off the deck and onto the parched grass in front of the house.

"Everybody at the mine in Ivittuut liked Iikkila," he said, pausing to light his cigarette. "She was kind to everyone, teased everyone, and listened whenever someone needed cheering up. She made the best raisin bread, and sweet bread rolls." Tuukula laughed. "It wasn't just her bosom that Eqqitsiaq fell for. Iikkila is a beautiful woman, inside and out."

"How did she collect the clippings?"

"She didn't."

Tuukula pointed at the water tank in the near distance and steered us towards it. The boys' cries together with Luui's shrill laugh echoed around the houses, amazing me that they still had energy to play, only to remember that Luui had slept most of the way in the boat.

"There were lots of Danes at the mine. Iikkila knew them all. She said the clippings started to come last year. Some of them are photocopies, as if whoever was sending them to her had to search for them first."

"She doesn't know who sent them?"

"*Naamik*," Tuukula said, with a shake of his head. Smoke spilled from his mouth as he finished his cigarette. "Only that they were sent from Denmark."

"So, whoever sent them…"

"Knew Haarløv," Tuukula said. "They either knew or guessed what he had done."

"Done what?"

Tuukula lifted his finger, pausing my thoughts as we reached the water pump. He took the hammer and slid the claw behind the clasp and padlock. Tuukula worked the hammer back and forth until the soft, weather-beaten wood started to give and the screws popped out of the clasp. He opened the door, then gestured at my utility belt as I reached for my flashlight.

The small blue structure was like many others in the towns and villages of Greenland. A push of a button released a measured amount of water into a bucket or jerry can. Three pushes, I knew, would fill a two-litre container, and the grille below it would catch the excess water. In winter, the grille would be thick with ice. A warm sleeve heated by electricity stopped the pipes from freezing in the harsh Greenland winter.

"There," Tuukula said, taking my hand to direct the beam of my flashlight. "You see where the water flows through the pipe?"

"Yes?"

"An extra bit of pipe connecting the two. I bet if we open that we'll find something."

"Find what?"

"A container. Something the water will run through, taking deposits of something with it."

"Like what?"

"Aluminium fluorides," Tuukula said. "Traces of cryolite. Things you could find in the mine, or a laboratory or a science classroom."

"Don't," I said, as Tuukula tapped the hammer against the pipe. "I want someone to look at it. We've already done enough, breaking into the pump room."

"Then you believe me?"

"I believe someone thinks something is going on. That person sent Iikkila articles to prove that Haarløv is against the building of aluminium smelters in Greenland."

"There has been a lot about it in the news," Tuukula said.

"Yes, but to suggest Haarløv has poisoned a community…"

"Fluorides are waste products of aluminium smelting."

"Yes," I said. "But we don't know that Haarløv has done anything."

"The answer is in that pipe," Tuukula said, tapping it with the hammer. "And Ansu recognised Haarløv. She would recognise him again."

"I understand. Then we need to go back to Nuuk to find him."

"He's not there. I checked the gymnasium website. There's no Haarløv on their list of employees. Even if he changed his name, none of the photos match the ones from articles."

This was a new side to Tuukula. I struggled to imagine him using the internet, knowing that he did not even have a mobile phone, let alone anything more sophisticated.

"I used the school library in Qaanaaq," he said, with a shrug. "Luui showed me how."

"Of course, she did," I said, enjoying the smile curling my lips. I could hear Luui's voice as the children drifted closer to the water pump.

"Haarløv is the missing person," Tuukula said. "Someone thinks he is responsible for what is happening in Ingnerssuit. We need to find him to prove it."

"We can't do that here," I said. "We need to leave."

My stomach flipped at the thought of sailing back to Nuuk, and I wondered if Tuukula was able to drive, or if I would have to take my turn in the stern.

"We eat, and then we leave," he said, gathering Luui into his arms as the boys pulled her around the side of the pumphouse.

Part 15

Keep the coast on your right. Tuukula's last words before he curled into the bow of the boat to sleep, played in my head on repeat, over and over, as the granite cliffs and thick fingers of rock reached into the black waters of the Labrador Sea. I perched my nose on the lip of the collar of my sailing suit, flashing wild stares at Luui as she lay between her father's knees, her head almost hidden in the deep recess of her hood. Tuukula snored, loud enough to be heard over the soft crash of the waves against the bow, as we pushed north through remarkably forgiving seas.

The commissioner had given me seventy-two hours, but I didn't think he intended for me to stay awake for every hour of the investigation. I blinked into the sea spray, wiping the water and a film of sea salt from my eyebrows as I steered around lumps of ice, quartering the waves as Tuukula had instructed, and staying clear of the unpredictable icebergs standing tall and looming over us.

The burr of the outboard motor, together with the vibration of the waves through the hull was hypnotic, disturbed by the occasional crash of a calving iceberg, jolting me awake each time I felt myself sagging. I kept my mind active with thoughts of the case – more of a manhunt than a missing persons case, although the similarities made it easier to justify the search.

Ivan Haarløv, the handsome activist with an agenda, was now linked – by a person or persons unknown – to a potential poisoning. I pressed my hand against the deep cargo pocket sewn into the right trouser leg of the sailing suit, nodding as I felt the reassuring size and shape of the bottle I had filled with Ingnerssuit water. I wasn't sure who, but I just knew that someone in Nuuk would be able to test it, setting in motion what I hoped would be a proper investigation, and not just a shaman with a hammer in the pumphouse.

The thought made me smile, especially as I realised that even magic had its limitations. Tuukula was no more able to break open the pipe than I was. *Although*, I thought, with a glance at the clear skies above me, *he has some sway with the weather.* I smiled at the thought of Tuukula swimming deep down into the ocean to comb the hair of Sassuma Arnaa, the mother of the sea, in return for clear skies and calm seas.

"But when did he do that?" I said aloud, drawing a smile from Luui.

She scrabbled across the deck of the boat, over the thwart seat, pausing as the belt from her sailing suit snagged on an exposed bolt, before flopping onto the deck by my feet. Luui took a moment to extract her hand from inside deep sleeves, then slid onto her knees to wrap her fingers around one of mine.

"We're on another adventure, Luui," I said, unzipping my collar to free my mouth to speak.

"Where will it take us this time?"

Luui smiled and pointed over her shoulder towards the bow of the boat.

"North," she said.

"To Nuuk."

"*Naamik*," she said, turning her head from side to side within her hood. "North of Nuuk." She stabbed her fingers into the wind until I nodded.

"Okay," I said. "Further north."

I just hoped we wouldn't be sailing all the way.

Part 16

Luui and I slept in the bow as Tuukula took over in the stern, sailing the long and narrow fibreglass boat under the midnight sun another few hours before arriving in Nuuk. Luui pressed her tiny bottom into my stomach as she curled into her preferred sleeping position, tugging my arm over her and holding onto my fingers all the way into the harbour. Tuukula woke us with a gentle bump of the bow against the dock, promising that he would meet me in *Katuaq* at midday.

I wiped sleep from my eyes and brushed salt from my cheeks before shrugging out of my sailing suit. I tucked the bottle of Ingnerssuit water into the pocket of my police jacket and climbed the ladder onto the dock. Luui waved from the boat and I smiled back before heading into town.

I tried to remember who was on shift, hoping that Atii was at the station, that she didn't have the late shift. I had less than twenty-four hours to find Ivan Haarløv and I could use all the help I could get. I just hoped that whatever tension there had been between us was now gone. There wasn't time to get upset over men – there never was.

I found Atii in the parking lot, just as she was climbing in behind the wheel of a patrol car. She paused, half inside the cab, and then stepped out, pulling me into a hug as soon as I was close enough.

"I thought I'd lost you, P," she said.

"I was coming back."

"You know what I mean."

I brushed at a twist of hair in her fringe, teasing it out as I smiled, nodding that I knew exactly what she meant, even if I wasn't quite ready to say the words.

"I need your help," I said, tugging the bottle from my jacket pocket. "And I could use a ride."

Atii hiked her thumb at the passenger seat, and said, "Get in. I'm supposed to pick up Sergeant Duneq, but he's running late. I'm free until he calls."

I cringed at the thought of running into Duneq, especially as the clock was still ticking, but shoved the thought to one side as Atii pulled out of the parking lot and into the street.

"Where to?"

"Nukissiorfiit," I said, with a wave of the bottle in my hand. "I need them to test this."

"Water? From where?"

"Ingnerssuit."

Atii frowned, then slowed the car to a stop by the side of the road.

"I thought you were working a missing persons case."

"I am. Sort of."

"And it has something to do with water?"

"Maybe," I said.

"You're not making any sense, P."

"Probably because I don't understand most of what I'm working on."

Atii pulled away from the side of the road and I brought her up to speed on what I knew and what I didn't.

"So, you're looking for a man who isn't missing, but who might be trying to hide," she said, as she parked outside the head office for Nukissiorfiit in Greenland.

"Yes."

"And the answer is in the water?"

"And their records," I said, with a nod to the main entrance.

Atii dipped her head as she thought, then paused to check a message that beeped into her phone. "It's Duneq," she said. "I have to pick him up. I can come back for you later."

"I'll call you." I opened the door, then paused to take another look at Atii. "We're back to normal, right?"

"You better believe it," she said, although there was a tiny fleck of something in her eye that suggested she still needed a little more time until things were completely back to normal. "Call me," she said, as I climbed out of the patrol car and closed the door.

"We don't test water here," the receptionist said, as I placed the bottle on the desk between us. "You'll have to send it to the DTU lab in Sisimiut."

"You can't do that?"

"Send it?"

"Yes," I said, with an exaggerated sigh. It wasn't hard to act tired, but adopting the role of exhausted police officer needing a break seemed to help.

"Leave it with me," she said.

"There is one more thing," I said, hoping that I wasn't pushing my luck.

"Just one more thing?"

"Yes."

"And what's that?"

I pulled my notebook from my jacket and tore a page out of it. I pulled my pen from my shirt pocket and printed Ivan Haarløv's name on the page.

"I'm looking for this man," I said. "He's Danish. I think he worked for Nukissiorfiit, at least two years ago. Could you search your personnel records, maybe give me a current address?"

"I'll have to run it by my supervisor."

"I understand," I said, as I added my name and phone number to the page with Haarløv's name. "If you could call and let me know."

"I'll see what I can do."

"Thank you."

I left the building as the receptionist answered an incoming call, pausing at the door as I caught my reflection in the glass. I looked tired, and, on closer inspection, crusty with sea salt.

"Perfect," I thought, as I walked out of the door.

I caught the bus back into town, daydreaming along *Sipisaq Kangilleq*, my forehead pressed against the cool window, before getting off at the stop by Nuuk Center, Greenland's only shopping mall.

The walk up to the gymnasium cleared my head, and I brushed the worst of the salt from my cheeks and my eyelashes before entering the modern glass and wood building. Students for the early classes were just arriving, and I slipped between them on my way up the stairs to the administration offices on the first floor. The rector, I discovered, was in a meeting, but I could wait in her office if I wanted to.

"Thanks," I said, before adding, "Could I wait with coffee?"

The woman behind the desk smiled and pointed the tip of a pencil at a coffee machine in the corner of her office.

"Help yourself," she said.

I took a large mug, filling it to just below the brim, before clutching it between salt-streaked hands. I let myself into the rector's office and slumped in a chair at a small round table in one corner of the room. I don't know how long I waited, only that she needed to squeeze my shoulder to wake me.

"Constable?"

"Yes?" I said, lifting my head, sloshing coffee, untouched, from my mug onto the table.

I looked up at a woman of medium height and of Danish origin. She sat down, adjusting her glasses and clearing a stack of papers to one side before pulling her chair closer to the table. "How can I help?"

"Ivan Haarløv," I said, spelling his name. "I think he used to work here. I'd like to ask him some questions but need to find him first. I was hoping you could help."

"Haarløv?" The rector tapped her chin with a long finger. "I don't remember anyone called

Haarløv, but Ivan rings a bell. He taught science, just for a short time, earlier this year. Ivan Linauskas. Not Haarløv."

I wrote the name in my notebook, pausing as the rector spelled it.

"Is it this man?" I pulled out my smartphone, opening the photo gallery and swiping my finger until I found the grainy image of Haarløv I had taken from one of the articles in Iikkila's scrapbook.

"Let me see." The rector took my phone, zoomed in with a pinch of her fingers, and said, "I'm not sure, but perhaps, if you gave him a moustache."

"Linauskas has a moustache?"

"He did when he worked here."

"And do you know where he is now?"

"I think he is in Aasiaat. They needed a science teacher, and I suggested he could try there." She stood up to walk to her desk, reaching for her phone. "I can call and check if you like."

"No," I said, rising from my seat. "Please don't."

"Are you sure? It's just a quick call."

"I'm sure," I said, suddenly concerned that as I got closer to finding Haarløv, the last thing I wanted to do was alert him that he was a person of interest. "You've been very helpful. I'll take it from here."

I called Atii as soon as I was out of the building, arranging to meet her at the station. I walked back towards the shopping mall, full of renewed energy that things were falling into place, albeit with the potential for mistaken identity ruining a positive identification. I checked the time on my phone, hoping that Tuukula and Luui would be on time, as I turned towards the café in *Katuaq*.

Part 17

Atii wasn't alone when I brought Tuukula and Luui to the station. She met us at the door, whispering a warning as she led us to one of the meeting rooms reserved for training and larger briefings. My stomach cramped when I saw Duneq scowl at me from his seat along the wall, and again when the commissioner walked across the room to greet Tuukula and Luui. Gaba, his arms folded across his chest, stood in front of the screen at the opposite end of the room.

"You're our shaman consultant," the commissioner said, as he shook Tuukula's hand.

"*Aap*," Tuukula said.

"I love how he owns it," Atii said, whispering into my ear.

Tuukula tousled Luui's hair once she had greeted the commissioner, sending her to the back of the room to wait as the meeting resumed.

"We've been busy since you called, Constable," the commissioner said, nodding for Gaba to continue as he rested against a desk.

Gaba stepped forward, squaring his feet as he brought everyone up to speed. In typical Gaba fashion, he snapped his fingers when he wanted Atii to change slides on the computer screen behind him. I stifled another smile as Luui made soft snaps of her own fingers to echo Gaba's. The SRU sergeant continued after a short beat of irritation.

"Local police have confirmed that Ivan Linauskas is currently residing in Aasiaat. They have his location." *Snap*. Gaba pointed at a small apartment block close to the harbour. "But don't have the resources to apprehend him."

Atii changed slides following a soft snap of fingers from the back of the room.

"Luui," Tuukula whispered, as Gaba took a sharp intake of breath.

"Magic," she said.

"*Aap*. But not now."

"Sergeant," the commissioner said, hiding his grin behind a mug of coffee. "If you'll carry on."

"Hmm," Gaba said. He nodded at Atii and waited for her to switch back to the previous slide before continuing. "Linauskas is here. Confirmed as of…" Gaba paused to check the chunky watch on his wrist. "One hour ago. The *King Air* is ready, and I suggest we leave within the next fifteen minutes."

"Who?" Duneq said, as he stood up. He thrust a fat finger in my direction, and then turned to point at Atii. "I need these two here, in Nuuk. Not flying halfway up the coast."

"George," Gaba said, throwing Duneq a look that pressed him back into his seat. "Constables Napa and Jensen were with me in Ingnerssuit. Linauskas is related to that investigation. I'm taking both of them with me to Aasiaat. We'll be back by this evening."

"And in the meantime, I have to change the duty roster, again," Duneq said. He turned to the commissioner, as if expecting him to make the final decision.

"I gave Petra seventy-two hours," the commissioner said. "She has until the end of the day. Sergeant Alatak promises to have her back in Nuuk by then. I'm deferring to Gaba's judgement on this."

"But she lied," Duneq said, rising again. He jabbed another finger at Tuukula, gesturing at the tuft on top of his head. "He fits the description of the missing man. Exactly."

Snap.

I looked at Gaba, then turned as he pointed to the back of the room.

"Petra found *ataata*," Luui said, followed by another *snap*. "Magic."

Duneq snorted, then jabbed his finger at me for the second time. "She's wasting police resources, Commissioner. I expect disciplinary action."

"That's enough, Sergeant," Gaba said.

"You don't tell me what to do or say, Gaba. Remember that."

"I will remember that." Gaba tucked his thumbs into his utility belt. "But in operational situations you need to remember that I have command. I'm taking Napa and Jensen with me to Aasiaat, together with Taatsiaq," he said, turning to the commissioner. "With your permission."

"Agreed." The commissioner placed his mug on the table before addressing the room. "Obviously, there are some details that need ironing out once this is over. But our first priority is finding Linauskas and bringing him in for a quiet chat.

Once we have him here in Nuuk, then," he said, with a nod to me and Sergeant Duneq, "any outstanding concerns will be resolved."

"I want her privileges revoked," Duneq said, bringing on another bout of cramps in my stomach.

"We'll see," the commissioner said. He turned to Tuukula and held out his hand. "I'm glad you were so easily found," he said, with a flash of amused light in his eye. "And I'm pleased we could finally meet."

"I need to go with them," Tuukula said.

"To Aasiaat?" The commissioner frowned. "I don't think that's necessary, or appropriate."

"It's my case." Tuukula turned to look at Duneq. "I made the call. I reported the missing person."

"He should go," Duneq said. "Take him with you."

For once, Duneq was difficult to read. I couldn't tell if it was spite or confusion, spurred on by the shaman in the room, that encouraged him to side with Tuukula. I waited as the commissioner mulled it over, avoiding Gaba's glare and the slow smile curling the side of Duneq's wide mouth.

"Fine," the commissioner said. "But if I might suggest, the girl stays here." He waved his hand as Tuukula started to speak. "Sergeant Duneq?"

"*Aap*?"

"Luui is your responsibility."

"Commissioner…"

Whatever Duneq might have said next was lost, the words stalled inside his mouth as the shaman's daughter clicked her tiny fingers.

Snap.

Part 18

The *King Air* flight, normally reserved for medical emergencies, bumped down on the runaway in Aasiaat just a few hours after the meeting ended with a snap of Luui's fingers. I might have enjoyed the thought of Sergeant Duneq looking after the shaman's daughter, but found myself preoccupied with the straps of another bulletproof vest, twisting and turning on the back seat of the Aasiaat police patrol car as we raced to the apartment block down by the harbour.

"Let me," Atii said.

"I'm never going to get the hang of this," I said, letting Atii make the final adjustments on my vest.

"You will," she said. "One day."

The local police officer slowed the patrol car, pulling in behind the taxi that carried Gaba and Taatsiaq. He pointed at the apartment block, a two-storey wooden building painted bright red. It was a stone's throw from the water, and a row of fibreglass dinghies and small trawlers bobbed in the water opposite the building.

"Let's go," Gaba said, rapping his knuckles on the window. "Not you," he said, as Tuukula got out of the car. Gaba pressed his palm against Tuukula's chest and nodded at the side of the road. "You wait here, until I tell you otherwise. Understand?"

Taatsiaq grinned from where he stood at the front of the patrol car, and I caught the look in his eye that could have been satisfaction. I wondered if he had forgiven Tuukula for stealing me away from the dance floor the night he arrived in Nuuk. I hadn't thought about it since, which confirmed that I didn't need to. I tugged the helmet onto my head, adjusted my ponytail and clicked the chinstrap closed.

"Ready," I said, as Gaba did a visual check of my gear.

"You'll be behind me," he said, clicking his fingers for Atii to turn around as he checked her vest. "You'll do what I say, or what Taatsiaq says – without question."

This seemed to be the part he enjoyed most, and I wondered what Atii saw in him, beyond his muscles, his square jaw, and... I stopped myself before I could go any further. It wasn't the time. I took a last look at Tuukula, flashing my hand in a discreet wave, before Atii whispered that I should take my pistol out of my holster.

I turned to follow her, impressed by the way she carried herself, as if this was something she could get used to, that she actually enjoyed. I wondered if Atii might be the first female officer to join the SRU. And then the thought was gone as I took my first step onto the stairs leading to the second floor of the apartment block.

Gaba stopped me at the top, pointing with two stiff fingers at the position he wanted me to take, against the corner of the building, with a good view of the stairs.

"Atii will be in front of you," he said. "Watch her back."

I intended to. I just hoped the sudden surge of adrenalin would settle so that I could hold my hands steady in the event that I had to use my pistol.

I didn't know how Gaba trained his SRU team, but I remembered how it was drilled into us that if we ever drew our pistol in the line of duty, it would likely be fast, that the situation would be – for lack of a better word – *messy*. Soldiers were trained to be efficient with their shots, putting bullets downrange to keep the enemy's head down, or assaulting a position, situations in which there was a tactical purpose to using their weapons. We were taught to use our weapons to stop a bad situation getting worse, often requiring quick actions with little time for finesse. I imagined Gaba and Taatsiaq operated someone in between the two extremes.

Gaba clicked his fingers, drawing my attention to his face and then back to his fingers as he held three of them up, counting down from *three, two…*

Taatsiaq kicked in the door as Gaba folded his last finger onto his fist.

I held my breath as Atii moved up to where Gaba had been standing, her pistol held in a steady two-handed grip, covering the door, as Gaba followed Taatsiaq inside Linauskas' apartment. I heard Taatsiaq's voice calling *Clear!* Followed by Gaba doing the same. Atii lowered her pistol as Gaba exited the apartment, talking into his radio, calling for the local police officer to come on up.

"Petra," Tuukula called up from the bottom of the stairs.

"What?"

"He's getting away."

Tuukula pointed out to sea, and I saw a small fibreglass dinghy, bow raising, as it powered out of the small harbour.

"Atii," I said, as I holstered my pistol. "Look."

I took two stairs at a time, thudding onto the gravel outside the apartment block, just as the local police officer brushed past me on his way up the stairs. I heard him curse, then turned to see Atii as she thundered down the stairs, calling out a quick apology as the police officer stepped smartly out of her way.

"Over here," Tuukula said. "Quickly."

I raced across the road with Atii right behind me. We both ignored Gaba's shouts for us to *wait* and the second one that threatened more than one kind of disciplinary action.

"No time," I said, slowing to follow Tuukula over the rocks between the road and the boats moored on the water below. He leaped into the nearest boat, and, before I could think about it, I followed him.

"Untie us," he said, as Atii thumped onto the deck. I caught her arm, grinning despite myself, as I reached for the rope tethering us to the land.

"Knife," Atii said, reaching around me to cut through the rope as Tuukula tugged the starting handle and the outboard roared into life.

Atii folded her knife back into her utility belt as I pushed away from the rocks. Tuukula put the motor into reverse, pulling away from the harbour just as Gaba appeared on the rocks above.

"Constable Jensen," he shouted, stabbing his finger at the water right below him.

"Sorry," I said, as Tuukula spun the boat in a tight turn. I gripped the gunwale as he accelerated, leaving Gaba on the shore shouting at Taatsiaq to *find a bloody boat.*

Atii squirmed her feet onto the deck, nodding at Tuukula as she pulled her pistol from her holster, checking the magazine and holding the pistol by her side as Tuukula increased speed.

Part 19

In the short space of just a few days, I had seen Atii look hurt, seen her jealous side, seen the confident, striking side of her as she dressed to impress, and now, in the bow of a stolen boat, I saw the strong young woman I had always known her to be, throwing off whatever insecurities she might have had, as she embraced the power that burned within her. She kept her arm straight, pointed directly at Linauskas' boat, calling out the distance, guiding Tuukula with one hand, her pistol gripped comfortably in the other. I made myself useful as ballast, shifting my weight under Tuukula's direction to trim the boat. Behind us, I could see Gaba, standing tall in a boat, hands folded across his chest as he waited for Taatsiaq to get the motor started.

I felt the rumble of my phone vibrating inside my jacket. I pulled it out and pressed it to my ear, turning my head out of the wind.

"This is Salaat from Nukissiorfiit. You wanted to know about Ivan Haarløv."

"Yes," I said. "Do you have an address?"

"He moved to Denmark, but one of my colleagues said he came back to Nuuk to teach."

"Thank you," I said. "That's very helpful." I ended the call, nodding to Atii that Nukissiorfiit had confirmed another piece of Ivan Haarløv's and Linauskas' story.

"Good," she said. "Because we're gaining on him. Get ready."

I turned away from Gaba, wondering for a moment just what we intended to do when we caught up with Linauskas, but also confident that he wouldn't run if he didn't have something to hide, giving me hope that I would be able to justify my actions to the commissioner, and to circumvent any action that Sergeant Duneq intended to take.

Of course, everything depended on what happened next, and when Linauskas slowed to pick up a rifle, I realised that the situation was about to change – drastically.

"Stay down," Atii said, pressing her hand on top of my helmet.

"Two guns are better than one," Tuukula said.

"And make a bigger target," she said.

Atii shifted her stance, anticipating the small waves from the wake of Linauskas' boat, raising her pistol in a two-handed grip, preparing to shoot.

Linauskas' first shot cracked above our heads, causing Atii to do little more than flinch, then bite her lip as she steadied her aim.

"A little closer," she said to Tuukula. "A little faster."

"Atii," I said, ducking as Linauskas fired for a second time.

"Not now, P," Atii said. "Concentrating."

She lifted her hands to aim, cursing as the boat bumped over a tiny wave. Then, with another bite of her lip, Atii fired.

"Again," she said, as her first shot plumed into the water just behind the outboard motor of Linauskas' boat. Atii pulled the trigger. Another plume of water. She fired again, cursed, then bit her lip so hard it turned white. "This time," she said, as she curled her finger around the trigger.

Atii's fourth shot slammed into the outboard motor, splintering the casing and punching a hole, out of which thick oily smoke pillowed around the dinghy. I heard Linauskas cough as Tuukula cut the power and we drifted towards him.

"Up, P," Atii said. "Draw your pistol."

I snapped the flap of my holster, remembering the last time I had pointed it at a man in the mountains of Kangaamiut, wondering why this week had been so different. It hit me then, as we approached. I was better at the unexpected, reacting to something, rather than planning for it. I stood next to Atii, bumping my shoulder against hers as Tuukula turned us in a wide arc around Linauskas' dinghy.

Atii called out for him to drop the rifle and he threw it over the side of the boat. I kept my eyes on him, ignoring the splash, but with one ear tuned to the sound of another boat approaching fast from Aasiaat.

"Gaba's on his way," Atii said, as Tuukula settled into a second circle around Linauskas. "Do you think he'll confess?"

"To poisoning the water?" I thought about it for a second, imagining that it would have a lot to do with the results of the water in Ingnerssuit, and whatever lay hidden inside the pipes of the pumphouse. "I hope so," I said. "For everyone's sake."

Tuukula pulled away, loitering to one side as Gaba and Taatsiaq moved in to arrest Linauskas. Atii holstered her pistol the second Gaba slapped a pair of handcuffs around Linauskas' wrists. I did the same, sighing as the adrenalin leaked out of my blood and my heart returned to a normal rhythm. Tuukula said nothing, not even when I asked how he was doing. He stared at Linauskas for what seemed like a minute, then pulled alongside the stricken dinghy to tow it back to Aasiaat.

"Let's go home," he said, as we followed Gaba's boat back to the harbour.

Part 20

Atii was the star of the show on the flight back to Nuuk, drawing praise from Taatsiaq and Gaba at her *incredible shot*, which she re-enacted for them several times before the captain of the *King Air* suggested we take our seats for landing. Linauskas said nothing, keeping his head down and avoiding everyone's eyes, especially Tuukula's.

"You're not going to say anything to him?" I asked Tuukula, as we tightened our seatbelts. "This is probably your last chance."

"There's nothing to say. He knows what he has done. He knows we know, and the results of the water will confirm it."

"But you don't want to ask him why?"

"I know why," Tuukula said, raising his voice. "He thought he was protecting the land, that he would use the people for the greater good. But he forgot something important, something you don't see in Denmark or the city." Tuukula leaned forward, closer to Linauskas. "What you forgot," he said, "is that in Greenland, the land *is* the people. They are one. You can't separate them, and you shouldn't pit them against each other. If you do that, nobody wins." Tuukula leaned back and settled in his seat. He took my hand, and said, "I have said what I needed to say. *Qujanaq.*"

We landed shortly after, with little more than a soft bump of the wheels and the whine of the engines as the captain taxied to the hangar. Taatsiaq took care of Linauskas, flashing me a grin as he left the plane. I followed Gaba and Atii onto the apron slowing to wait for Tuukula as he climbed down the short aircraft steps.

"We're going to *Mattak* tonight," Atii said. "SRU tradition."

"That's okay," I said. "I need my bed."

"Taatsiaq is going."

"I know, but I'm tired. Maybe another time."

"Okay." Atii pulled me into a tight hug, then loosened the Velcro tabs of my vest. "Are you riding with us back to the station?"

"No," I said, as Tuukula joined us. "I think we'll go to the hospital first. I'll see you later, or tomorrow."

I waited for Atii and Gaba to leave, wondering if we would need a taxi before I remembered that Sergeant Duneq was still looking after Luui.

"There she is," Tuukula said, as we walked to the airport building.

He waved as Luui pressed her face against the window, blowing air out of her cheeks and smearing the glass. Sergeant Duneq stood just behind her, alternating between a stern look in my direction and a softer one aimed at Luui.

"You shouldn't be too hard on the Sergeant," Tuukula said.

"Me? Too hard on *him*?"

"*Aap*. He is a good man, even though it might be difficult to see it sometimes."

"A good man? Really?"

"I wouldn't leave Luui with anyone I didn't trust," Tuukula said. He crouched as Luui bolted through the door and into his arms.

I nodded at Sergeant Duneq, waiting for him to say something, but, in that moment at least, training was over, and he had nothing more to say. I waved as he turned to leave, only to see him stagger as Luui raced from her father's arms to grab Duneq's leg. She extended her hand to give him a proper handshake, then ran back to Tuukula as Duneq turned to leave.

"Wait," I said, just as Duneq walked out of view. "We should have got a lift to the hospital."

"No need," Tuukula said, nodding at the commissioner as he pulled up outside the airport in his personal car.

"Get in," the commissioner said, as he rolled down the window. He waited until Tuukula and Luui were settled in the back, and I climbed into the passenger seat. "I agreed with Sergeant Duneq that I would pick you up. It'll give us a chance to talk before you start your next shift tomorrow."

"Am I in trouble, Sir?"

"With me? Not at all."

"And with Sergeant Duneq?"

"Always." The commissioner laughed. "But before we get into that, I thought you should know that Nukissiorfiit sent a crew from Paamiut to check the water pump in Ingnerssuit. They found an empty container with walls like a sieve that has some residue inside it. They'll be processing that along with more water samples."

"Is that enough to prove that Linauskas poisoned the water?" Tuukula asked.

"It might be, if anyone can confirm that he was in Ingnerssuit."

"Ansu can," I said. "Eqqitsiaq's daughter."

"Good," the commissioner said. "Which is useful, as we're flying everyone in Ingnerssuit up to Nuuk for tests. They'll be here tomorrow."

The commissioner braked for a traffic light and we carried on in silence until he parked outside the main entrance to Dronning Ingrid's Hospital.

"I won't come in," he said, as we got out of the car. "But, Constable..."

"Yes?"

"Good work." The commissioner smiled, then waved as he pulled away.

"Your vest," Tuukula said, as we entered the hospital.

"Right," I said, fiddling with the straps until I could remove it.

I hooked it over my arm as we climbed the stairs to the first floor. Tuukula slowed as we approached the ward, falling silent the closer we got to Eqqitsiaq's room. We stopped outside the door, and I pressed my hand on Tuukula's shoulder, encouraging him to go inside with a dip of my head. He nodded and pushed the door open. I started to follow him, only to feel Luui curl her hand around my finger and tug me gently, but insistently, back into the corridor.

"Old magic," she said, with a nod to the door. "Too old for you and me."

"What magic?" I said, as Luui and I found a

seat.

"Friendship," she said.

Luui swung her feet as she sat on the chair, her eyes fixed on the door to Eqqitsiaq's room, and her hand curled around my fingers. I sank back in the chair, feeling the weight of the bulletproof vest on my thighs, and something else, heavier, tugging at my eyelids, suggesting that now, with nothing else more pressing to do, I could finally go to sleep.

The End

About the Author

Christoffer Petersen is the author's pen name. He lives in Denmark. Chris started writing stories about Greenland while teaching in Qaanaaq, the largest village in the very north of Greenland – the population peaked at 600 during the two years he lived there. Chris spent a total of seven years in Greenland, teaching in remote communities and at the Police Academy in the capital of Nuuk.

Chris continues to be inspired by the vast icy wilderness of the Arctic and his books have a common setting in the region, with a Scandinavian influence. He has also watched enough Bourne movies to no longer be surprised by the plot, but not enough to get bored.

You can find Chris in Denmark or online here:

www.christoffer-petersen.com

By the Same Author

THE GREENLAND CRIME SERIES
featuring Constable David Maratse
SEVEN GRAVES, ONE WINTER Book 1
BLOOD FLOE Book 2
WE SHALL BE MONSTERS Book 3
INSIDE THE BEAR'S CAGE Book 4
WHALE HEART Book 5

Short Stories from the same series

KATABATIC
CONTAINER
TUPILAQ
THE LAST FLIGHT
THE HEART THAT WAS A WILD GARDEN
QIVITTOQ
THE THUNDER SPIRITS
ILULIAQ
SCRIMSHAW
ASIAQ
CAMP CENTURY
INUK
DARK CHRISTMAS
POISON BERRY
NORTHERN MAIL
SIKU

VIRUSI
THE WOMEN'S KNIFE
ICE, WIND & FIRE

THE GREENLAND TRILOGY
featuring Konstabel Fenna Brongaard
THE ICE STAR Book 1
IN THE SHADOW OF THE MOUNTAIN Book 2
THE SHAMAN'S HOUSE Book 3

MADE IN DENMARK
Short Stories featuring Milla Moth set in Denmark
DANISH DESIGN Story 1

THE POLARPOL ACTION THRILLERS
featuring Sergeant Petra "Piitalaat" Jensen,
Etienne Gagnon, Hákon Sigurðsson & more
NORTHERN LIGHT Book 1
MOUNTAIN GHOST Book 2

THE DETECTIVE FREJA HANSEN SERIES
set in Denmark and Scotland
FELL RUNNER Introductory novella
BLACKOUT INGÉNUE

THE WOLF CRIMES SERIES
set in Denmark, Alaska and Ukraine
PAINT THE DEVIL Book 1
LOST IN THE WOODS Book 2
CHERNOBYL WOLVES Book 3

THE WHEELMAN SHORTS
Short Stories featuring Noah Lee set in Australia

PULP DRIVER Story 1

THE DARK ADVENT SERIES
featuring Police Commissioner
Petra "Piitalaat" Jensen set in Greenland
THE CALENDAR MAN Book 1
THE TWELFTH NIGHT Book 2
INVISIBLE TOUCH Book 3
NORTH STAR BAY Book 4

UNDERCOVER GREENLAND
featuring Eko Simigaq and Inniki Rasmussen
NARKOTIKA Book 1

CAPTAIN ERRONEOUS SMITH
featuring Captain Erroneous Smith
THE ICE CIRCUS Book 1

THE BOLIVIAN GIRL
a hard-hitting military and political thriller series
THE BOLIVIAN GIRL Book 1

GUERRILLA GREENLAND
featuring Constable David Maratse
ARCTIC STATE Novella 1
ARCTIC REBEL Novella 2

GREENLAND MISSING PERSONS novellas
featuring Constable Petra "Piitalaat" Jensen
THE BOY WITH THE NARWHAL TOOTH
THE GIRL WITH THE RAVEN TONGUE
THE SHIVER IN THE ARCTIC
THE FEVER IN THE WATER

Made in United States
Orlando, FL
22 January 2022